# SEA QUEST

# TRAGG
## THE ICE BEAR

*With special thanks to Brandon Robshaw*

www.seaquestbooks.co.uk

ORCHARD BOOKS
338 Euston Road, London NW1 3BH
*Orchard Books Australia*
Level 17/207 Kent St, Sydney, NSW 2000

A Paperback Original
First published in Great Britain in 2014

Sea Quest is a registered trademark of Beast Quest Limited
Series created by Beast Quest Limited, London

Text © Beast Quest Limited 2014
Cover and inside illustrations by Artful Doodlers,
with special thanks to Bob and Justin © Orchard Books 2014

A CIP catalogue record for this book is available from
the British Library.

ISBN 978 1 40832 863 7

1 3 5 7 9 10 8 6 4 2

Printed in Great Britain by CPI Group (UK) Ltd, Croydon, CR0 4YY

Orchard Books is a division of Hachette Children's Books,
an Hachette UK company

www.hachette.co.uk

# TRAGG
## THE ICE BEAR

## BY ADAM BLADE

ORCHARD

I'm coming for you, Max!

You think you have defeated me -
the mighty Cora Blackheart? Idiot
boy! You've only made me angry!
I may have lost my ship and my
crew, but it's not over. Now it's
just you and me...and the deadly
Robobeasts under my control!

You have something that I want, Max
- an object so powerful, I can use
it to rule all of Nemos! And you
don't even know it...

But first I will destroy your
whole family - your mother, your
father...and that irritating Merryn
girl, too.

Cora Blackheart will have her
revenge!

# CHAPTER ONE

# THE CHASE BEGINS

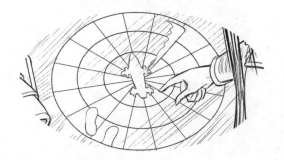

The *Leaping Dolphin* moved slowly through the dark water of the Lost Lagoon, chugging along in fits and starts. It was easy for Max, swimming alongside, to keep pace.

He had left the submarine to check on the damage to its hull. Their recent battle with Cora Blackheart and Rekkar the Screeching Orca had taken its toll. The metal exterior was speckled with lumpy black rock from an

underwater volcanic eruption, and the crust of lava had sealed up all the rips and holes that the *Leaping Dolphin* had suffered in the battle. Still, it looked terrible.

*More like the Limping Dolphin*, Max thought grimly. The added weight of the rock was slowing the sub down, and its power had been low to start with.

Rivet, Max's robot dog, rubbed up against his leg. "Fix, Max. Fix!"

"I wish I could, boy," Max said, scratching the dogbot's metal head.

*Cora had better not catch up with us any time soon*, he thought. *We'd have no chance, with the submarine in this state.*

Max shivered. They were moving steadily northward from the sandy island they had first landed on in the Lost Lagoon, and the water was getting colder. But at least they were putting distance between themselves and Cora.

"Feeling a bit chilly, Max?" said Lia, grinning, as she rode up on her swordfish, Spike. She had been scouting out in front to see what lay ahead in the gloomy water. "This is nothing. You want to try spending a winter underwater in Sumara. Then you'd know what cold is!"

"Did you see anyone, Lia?" Max's mother's voice sounded in their headsets. "We need to find those metals, remember?"

*And quickly*, thought Max. They already had some Galdium, but they needed three more rare metals – Rullium, Ferrum and Barrum. Then they'd be able to build a compass that would get them out of the Lost Lagoon.

Lia frowned. "No. But I did see some icebergs."

"Icebergs?" Max's mum's voice became urgent. "You'd both better come back inside. It won't be easy to get past them, with the sub in this state. I could do with a set of Merryn eyes in here."

"Do I have to?" Lia grumbled. "I hate being stuck between those metal walls, when I could be out in the great wide ocean!"

Max tried to persuade her. "Come on, Lia

– it's only till we get past the icebergs."

Lia pouted. "Oh, all right." She patted Spike's head. "See you soon, Spike! Stay close."

Max swam to the top of the sub and unscrewed the hatch. He climbed through the airlock, followed by Rivet, while Lia strapped on her Amphibio mask so she could breathe air.

"Good," said Max's mother. "Now hold on tight. This could be a bumpy ride."

The interior of the sub was narrow and dimly lit. The flask of Galdium stood on a shelf, shining in the gloom.

"Can't we turn the lights up?" Max asked.

His mother shook her head. "We're running on backup power. There's barely enough energy to keep the sub moving and run the navigation system."

The low light glinted off the green brooch

she wore. Their pirate friend Roger had given her that brooch, to replace the necklace Cora Blackheart had stolen from her.

*It's so good to spend time with Mum, after all these years apart*, Max thought. *I just wish we weren't in such a desperate situation.* But then his mother didn't seem to mind desperate situations too much. In fact, from the way her eyes gleamed with excitement, Max could tell she thrived on them. Just like him.

He stood beside his mum, and watched the line sweep round the radar screen. It wasn't picking anything up so they couldn't be that close to the icebergs yet.

Lia was standing near the front of the sub, gazing out of the porthole. Max went and joined her. There was nothing out there except an expanse of dark green water, and the slightly darker shape of Spike swimming a little way ahead.

"How far away were those icebergs?" Max asked.

Lia shrugged. "A short swim. But Spike's a lot faster than this broken-down sub!"

*Blip-blip.*

Max turned as the bleeping noise broke the silence.

*Blip-blip.*

It was coming from the radar screen.

"Uh-oh," said Max's mum.

"What is it?" asked Max.

His mother pointed to the screen. Two dark shapes showed up, every time the line swept past.

"Is it the icebergs?" said Lia, squeezing up beside Max.

"It can't be," Max's mum said. "These things are behind us. Plus...they're moving!"

"And fast," Max said. "As fast as an aquabike.

Big, too. Could they be...Robobeasts?" He
felt a prickle of worry. *This sub's in no state to
face anything...let alone a pair of Robobeasts.*

"Could be," his mum said. "And with our
power so low, I don't fancy our chances of
losing them."

"Then we'll have to take them on," Max said,
feeling determination well up in his chest.
He'd been hoping that Cora wouldn't catch

up with them while their sub was damaged. But now it looked as if her Robobeasts were on their tail, and they had no choice but to fight. Their chances weren't good, Max knew, but if they could somehow outwit them... This could be a chance to defeat Cora once and for all!

"How can we?" Lia demanded. "The blaster cannons don't work. Even your hyperblade is bent. We don't have any weapons to fight with!"

Max knew she was right. *But there must be a way!* He turned to his mum. "Can't we get the weapons system up and running?"

"Let me see what I can do," said his mum. She went to the console and stabbed at some buttons. Max knew what she was doing – diverting all the power that could be spared to the sub's weaponry.

*Blip-blip.*

*Blip-blip-blip-blip!*

The bleeps were getting faster. And Max knew that meant their pursuers were getting closer...

The submarine slowed down and the lights dimmed even further, as the weapons system panel on the console lit up.

"Yesss!" said Max and his mother at exactly the same time.

The panel flickered and went dark.

Max and his mother groaned.

*Blip-blip-blip-blipblipblip!*

"Look, Max! Max, look!"

Rivet was at the back of the sub, his paws pressed against the porthole, looking out.

Through the glass, Max saw two huge black shadows looming behind them, getting closer and closer.

Max felt a cold hand of dread clutch his stomach. They should have used all their power to get away. *It would be hard enough for us to fight one Robobeast*, he thought. *But two? We're done for...*

# CHAPTER TWO

# ATTACK OF
# THE SEA WORM

"Quick!" said Max. "Can we power the engine back up?"

His mother's fingers flickered over the console. The engine note rose, and Max felt the sub speed up.

Slightly.

*Not enough*, Max thought. The bleeps from the radar were getting faster all the time.

"I can see the icebergs!" Lia shouted. Max looked ahead, and saw a number of pale shapes glimmering in the dark water.

"I'll steer between them!" Max's mother said. "Maybe I can shake off the Robobeasts."

"What about Spike?" Lia said desperately. "He's out there on his own!"

"He can look after himself, Lia," said Max. He just hoped it was true.

As the first iceberg rushed towards them, Max's mum spun the steering wheel to one side. Max felt his lungs squeeze as the icy surface passed just a fin's length away. They sped past the berg, somehow managing to only graze it. Through the portholes on one side of the sub, everything turned white.

*If we hit an iceberg full on, this sub will crumple like a tin can*, Max thought.

*Bleepbleepbleepbleepbleeeeeeep...*

Lia gasped as another berg loomed up, and Max's mum spun the wheel the other way. The sub zigzagged from side to side as she steered first left, then right. Max had to hold onto a shelf to avoid being thrown all over the place. The rock-covered sides of the sub made a sickening grinding noise as they scraped the ice, but again, the *Leaping Dolphin* made it through.

*Bleeeeeeeeeep!*

The Robobeasts were nearly upon them. Max didn't dare turn to look properly. *They'll rip the sub apart*, Max thought, trying to plan ahead. *We'll have to swim clear*. There was no danger of drowning – the water was Lia's natural element, of course, and both Max and his mother had received the Merryn Touch, so they could breathe underwater too. But the Robobeasts would come after them. *If we have to die, we'll die fighting*, Max thought, pulling out his hyperblade. But it was bent out of shape, with a blunted edge. *I suppose it's better than nothing*, Max thought.

*But not much better.*

*Blip-blip-blip-blip...*

"Hey!" Lia said. "Sounds like they're slowing down."

"You're right!" Max said.

*Blip-blip. Blip-blip.*

He went to look out of the rear porthole, supporting himself against the side of the sub. The two black shapes were dwindling into the distance. Soon all Max could see was the dark, greyish water.

"They've given up!" Max said. "I wonder why?"

"Maybe they can't follow us here," Max's mother said, slowing the sub and steering through a narrow gap between two great cliffs of ice. "They're too big. *Leaping Dolphin One*, Robobeasts Nil, I'd say! Hey, this is fun!" Now the danger was over she seemed a bit light-headed. Max saw Lia trying to stifle a laugh at his mother's excitement.

"Mum, we have no weapons and we nearly got attacked by two Robobeasts at once!" he said. "That's not what I call fun!"

"We got away, didn't we?" Max's mother answered. "I missed stuff like this when I was cooped up on that island. It's great to be sharing an adventure with you, Max. It's just a shame your dad isn't here."

"Callum!" barked Rivet.

"That's right, boy," Max said, patting his back. "But I don't like thinking of Dad back in Aquora... He'll think the city is safe, now that the Professor's in prison. We have to get out of this Lagoon before Cora does, or she'll be able to launch a surprise attack with her Robobeasts!"

Lia picked up the container of Galdium. When Max had taken it from the volcano it had been red-hot and molten, but it had hardened into a shimmering blue crystal. "One down, three to go," Lia said.

"That's right," Max's mother said. "Now that we're out of danger, Max, try looking up Rullium in Rivet's database."

Max kneeled down beside Rivet and unscrewed the panel in his side.

Rivet jumped. "Tickles, Max!"

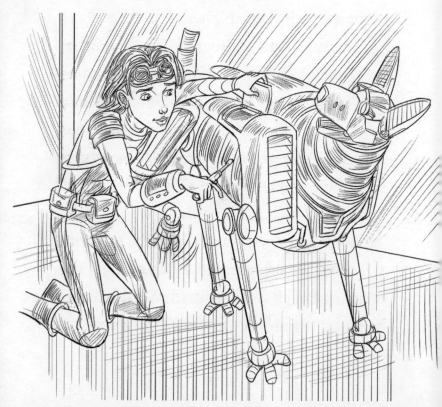

"Keep still!" Max told him. Under the panel was a screen. Max had programmed the database with the contents of the encyclopaedia from the Aquoran Central Library. He keyed in "Rullium" and the information appeared onscreen.

"*Rullium*," he read out. "*A rare mineral chiefly found in icy regions, and especially in glaciers.*"

"That's what I thought," Max's mother said, as she continued to steer the *Leaping Dolphin* between giant icy cliff faces. "We're in the right area, then. Once we have the Rullium we're halfway there, and once we've built the compass we'll be out of this Lagoon in no—"

The submarine rocked violently. Lia went staggering from one end of the sub to the other, Max fell over Rivet, and his mother had to hold onto the controls to stay upright.

"What's happening?" shouted Lia.

*Shhhloomph! Shhhloomph! Shhhloomph!*

A horrible sucking sound was coming from outside the sub. It gave Max a sick feeling in his stomach.

He looked out of the porthole and saw something. A long, snakelike shape flickered past. There was no sign of Spike. *Uh-oh.*

The sub rocked again. *Creeeeeaaaaaak...* The ceiling groaned as though some huge weight had settled on top of it.

Max looked up and with a jolt he saw water trickling from the metal roof. It was only a tiny crack – but if it got any bigger...

His mother was wrestling with the wheel. "I can hardly – control it!" she panted.

"I'm going out there!" Max said. Whatever strange Lost Lagoon creature was attacking them, he had to fight it off. He rushed towards the exit hatch, Rivet at his heels. But

Lia got there before him.

"I'm coming, Spike!" she yelled.

Max followed her up through the hatch. As soon as he got out into the water he gasped at the cold. It gripped him like a vice.

Then he saw what was on top of the submarine, and gasped again.

It was some kind of creature... An enormous sea worm. It had a ridged, muscular body, and two flat black discs for eyes. It was lying on top of the sub and seemed to be feeding on the volcanic rock. It chewed greedily at the lava with a horrible mouth, ringed with teeth.

*Shhhloomph! Shhhloomph! Shhhloomph!*

As it swallowed, Max could actually see the chunks of rock passing through its pale, slimy body.

"That's disgusting!" Lia said. "Is it a Robobeast?" Spike was swimming by her

side, his eyes wide with fear.

Max couldn't see any signs of robotic attachments on the animal. "I don't think so. But it's still dangerous."

*If we don't stop it*, he thought, *it'll eat away all the protective rock covering – and the Leaping Dolphin will flood.*

The sub was still moving, as Max's mum

struggled to steer between the walls of ice. Her voice came over Max's headset. "What's happening? I can't manage the wheel!"

"There's a creature on the sub – I'm going to try and get it off!" Max said.

The sub veered towards an iceberg, and Max imagined his mother desperately fighting to control it. He swam up to the sea worm and slashed at it with his hyperblade. Blunt as it was, the blade managed to sink into the creature's slimy body, clanging against a piece of rock it had swallowed. But when Max withdrew the blade, it hadn't even left a mark.

The sea worm carried on chewing away at the lava.

Suddenly Max heard a loud grating noise that set his teeth on edge. The sub had scraped against an iceberg, and the impact made the escape hatch door buckle. Max dived towards it and tried to open it, but it wouldn't budge. *No!* Now he and Lia couldn't get back into the sub.

Worse, his mother couldn't get out.

"Can't you use your Aqua Powers on it?" he shouted to Lia.

"I'm trying!"

Lia and Spike were swimming beside the worm. Lia's face creased in concentration as she tried to send her thoughts into its mind, but the sea worm continued to chomp mindlessly at the rock.

Max swam up close. He hated touching such a slimy creature, but he forced himself to put both arms around it and try to drag it away. Its skin felt soft and clammy, but muscular, and he could feel the sharp edges of rocks below the skin.

He tugged with all his strength.

But nothing happened. The creature was

way too strong.

To his horror, Max saw that it had eaten away a patch of hardened lava that had covered a split in the *Leaping Dolphin*'s hull. Water was beginning to flow in.

*If I don't do something fast*, he thought, *the sub will sink all the way to the ocean bed – with Mum trapped inside!*

# CHAPTER THREE

# KIDNAPPED BY SPIDERS

Max put his feet on the sea worm's body and tried to wrench it upwards with both hands. It still wouldn't budge.

"Rivet help!" barked the dogbot. It swam up and sank its metal jaws into the creature's body. The worm writhed a little, but held fast.

"If I can't use my Aqua Powers," Lia said, "let's see what I can do with my hands!"

She swam towards the sea worm and pummelled its head, hard, with both fists.

For a moment the creature stopped chewing the lava. *Perhaps the head is the most sensitive part*, Max thought. The sea worm turned to stare at Lia. Then, with startling speed, it rose from the sub and coiled around her, once… twice…three times, until only her head and legs could be seen. The coils tightened.

Lia screamed. "Ouch! The rocks inside it – they're crushing me, Max!"

"Hold on, Lia!" Max shouted. He had to save her! *But how?*

His mother's voice crackled in the headset. "Max! The water's coming in – I'm sinking!"

Max swallowed hard. Once the sub settled on the seabed, full of water, how would they ever raise it again? And the exit hatch wouldn't open. His mother would be stuck inside.

*Who should I save first?* he thought desperately. *Lia, or my mother?*

Lia cried out in pain. Max could see the

creature's coils tightening even further. The Merryn girl's eyes looked as if they were popping out of her head. *She's in greater danger*, Max realised.

"Hold on, Mum!" Max said into the headset. "Try to plug the gaps!" He swam towards Lia and tried to get his hand under the sea worm's coils to ease the pressure. No chance. The surface of its skin was soft, but its muscles were like iron.

Rivet was still biting the sea worm's body. But it didn't even seem to notice.

"Spike!" shouted Max. "Use your sword – cut Lia free!" He wasn't sure if the fish understood, so he pretended his arm was a swordfish bill, pointing at the sea worm.

Spike seemed to get the message. Rotating his fins, he drew back – then shot straight at the sea worm, slicing into its body with his razor-sharp bill.

Max couldn't believe his eyes. In seconds, Spike had sawn the creature clean in two.

"You did it, Spike!" said Max.

The sea worm's two halves fell away from Lia. There was no blood, Max noticed – each half just ended in a wall of white gristle.

"Yuck!" said Lia. She rubbed her bruised body, swimming away from the two limp, floating worm-pieces. "Thanks, Spike." She hugged the swordfish. "That was close!"

Max's headset came to life again.

"I think the *Leaping Dolphin*'s safe again – at least for now," his mother said. "I plugged up the holes with a spare tarpaulin."

"Nice work!" said Max. Now they needed to get out of this place, and find somewhere they could safely patch up the sub.

"Max!" Rivet barked. "Look!"

Max turned and saw the two halves of the sea worm twitching. His mouth dropped open. *Not dead yet?* he wondered. Then his stomach crawled as he saw two black discs appear on the eyeless half. Then a mouth-hole appeared, ringed with sharp teeth.

"It's coming back to life!" cried Lia.

*And now there are two of them!* Max's heart pounded as the worms came towards them.

"Backs against the sub!" Max said. "So they can't coil round us!"

He and Lia set their backs to the wall of the

*Leaping Dolphin*, with Spike and Rivet by their sides. The sea worms approached, opening their circular, teeth-ringed mouths. One went for Max, the other for Lia.

*Uh-oh…*

Max struck out with his blunted hyperblade again, aiming for the head. But the sea worm seemed to be ready. It ducked under the blow, then tried to fasten its teeth on Max. Max swerved away, but the sea worm's jaws closed on his wetsuit, grazing his skin. He managed to pull free, leaving a strip of fabric in the creature's mouth. Rivet's jaws clamped onto the worm's side, but it shook the dogbot off.

Lia was trying to fight off the other sea worm. Spike came to her aid, slicing it in half. But then the two smaller halves came to life at once and attacked Lia again.

"Stop it, Spike!" Lia shouted. "You're only making it worse!"

But Spike seemed too excited to hear her. He lunged at the worm that was attacking Max, and slashed that one in half too.

*Now four worms are attacking us!*

It was all Max could do to fend them off. He had to keep moving, pushing them away. But how much longer could they keep this up?

Before they could stop him, Spike attacked again. Soon there were eight wriggling, biting worms. Four continued the attack, while the others began gobbling up the lava on the sub.

*Oh no! They'll undo Mum's repairs!*

"Stop Spike doing that!" Max shouted.

"Spike! Stop!" Lia yelled. But the swordfish didn't even pause. "I can't get through to him – he's panicking!" Lia said.

"Get away from there!" Max's mother's voice said in his ear. "There are too many of those worms to fight!"

*She must be able to see what's happening*

*through the porthole*, Max realised. *But if we run, there's nothing to stop the sea worms eating the lava and sending the sub to the bottom.*

"I'm not going to leave you, Mum!" he said.

"You have to! Or we'll all die!"

"I'm not leaving you!" he repeated, as he hit one of the sea worms that was trying to bite his leg. *Not when I've just got you back…*

Then he saw that the sub was sinking again. The sea worms had chewed away the lava that had sealed the holes, and water flooded in.

*THWUMP!*

Right in front of Max, eight huge legs landed on the hull of the sub. They were long and white, and jointed like insect legs. Max looked up and saw that the legs belonged to a gigantic white spider, with a smooth, round body and shining mandibles.

"What?" Max said aloud. It was like some dreadful dream. Was this a giant ocean crawler, like the ones that took his mum away all those years ago? *Or worse…*

Suddenly, out of the corner of his vision, Max noticed a sea worm darting straight at his face. He turned just in time to see its tooth-ringed mouth open wide – but before it could reach him, a stream of silk shot from the spider's body and jerked it away.

Max was stunned. *Is the spider our friend?*

More of the giant white sea spiders were gathering now, looming out of the water like ghosts. Some landed on the sub, others hovered nearby. They all shot out lines of spider-silk, trapping the sea worms and tying them up in little bundles. A few spiders even went below the sub and began to push it back up towards the surface.

Max and Lia looked at each other, and Max saw his own confusion reflected in her face.

"What's going on?" Lia said.

Max shrugged as he put away his hyperblade. With a shock, he felt a strand of spider silk wrap itself around his middle. It was soft, but as strong as steel. The spider didn't wrap him up like it had with the sea worms, though. Max felt himself being pulled up through the water and flipped onto the giant spider's back. It started to swim.

"Wait, where are you taking me?" he cried out, but the spider didn't reply. Max felt the current rush against his face as the spider's long legs gracefully swished through the water.

Max looked back and saw Lia, Rivet and Spike being carried in the same way. Four spiders were even tugging the *Leaping Dolphin* along on silken threads.

"Can you speak to them with your Aqua Powers?" Max called to Lia.

"They still don't work," Lia said. "This stupid Lost Lagoon!"

"What's happening?" Max's mother's voice said in his ear. "Are you all right, Max?"

The spiders were taking them closer to the surface. In the distance, Max saw the dark shape of a landmass.

"I'm fine, Mum," Max said. "We've just been captured by some giant spiders, that's all..."

# CHAPTER FOUR

# THE ISLAND OF ILLUSION

Max felt his stomach lurch as the legs of the spider carrying him met solid ground. It sped up, scurrying onto a shore. Max's head broke the surface as he bounced on the spider's back. He shook the water from his face and craned his neck to see a pebbly beach, covered in glittering ice. In the far distance was a shimmering white haze. Mountains, perhaps.

*What is this place?*

Other spiders were scuttling up the beach, two of them carrying Lia and Rivet. There was no sign of the *Leaping Dolphin* yet. With a jolt Max saw Lia gasping vainly for breath. Her face was turning blue as she struggled to reach her Amphibio mask. But the spider silk held her firmly in place.

"She needs to breathe!" Max said to his spider. "Let her go so she can get her mask!"

The spider didn't seem to understand. Max waved and pointed at Lia. At last it seemed to get the message. One of its limbs rose up and a pincer snipped through Lia's bonds. She jumped to the ground, snatched the Amphibio mask that was tied to her belt and pulled it on, taking several deep, grateful breaths in quick succession.

"Are you OK, Lia?" Max called.

Lia gave him a thumbs-up sign, still breathing hard.

Max's spider snipped him free with a pincer and he slid down, wet and shivering with cold.

The spider that had carried him reared up on its four back legs. The four upper legs dangled by its sides, like arms, and suddenly it looked almost like a giant person – twice as tall as a man and with too many limbs.

Rivet landed on the ice beside Max. The dogbot's metal feet slid all over the place on the icy stones.

"Slippy, Max! Slidey!"

Max heard a crunching sound. Looking up the beach, he gasped as he saw a small army of the giant white spiders marching towards them. Their four upper limbs held swords and spears – gripped in their pincers – that glinted in the pale sunlight.

"Quite a reception committee," Max said quietly to Lia.

Rivet, still slipping around on the ice, started barking furiously at the spider-soldiers.

"Be quiet, Riv!" Max said. "We really don't want to get on the wrong side of these people." *If "people" is the right word*, he thought.

The spider army came to a halt just in front of them. They stood stock still, rank upon rank of heavily armed giants. Silent. Waiting.

Spike was jumping out of the water, making a whistling noise as if trying to attract Lia's attention.

"It's all right, Spike!" Lia called. "The spiders are friendly – I think," she added in a whisper to Max.

Max nodded. "Maybe. They let you get your mask, after all." Then he saw four more spiders emerge from the sea, towing the

*Leaping Dolphin* by silk ropes. The spiders dragged it up onto the beach, its metal hull screeching as it ground across the icy pebbles.

"Mum?" Max said into the headset. "Are you OK?"

There was a pause. Then his mother's voice came through. "I think so. I've been jolted about quite a bit and bumped my head. Where are we?"

"On land," Max said. "Come and see!"

"I'd love to…but I can't get out, remember?"

Max ran to the exit hatch and tried to open it. Lia came to help, but it still wouldn't budge.

The spider that had carried Max came over. It bent down, took the exit door in two of its steely pincers, and twisted. There was a grating noise and the door sprang open.

Max's mother climbed out, looking dishevelled, her hair hanging over her face.

She started when she saw the massed ranks of giant spiders.

"It's all right, Mum," Max said. "They're friends, I think. They rescued us."

"Good job I'm not scared of spiders!" Max's mother said. "Phew! I really didn't have a clue what was happening back there – I thought I was a goner!" She hugged Max, and then Lia.

The spiders were still watching silently, waiting.

"What do you think they want?" whispered Lia.

One of the spiders stood a little ahead of the rest. It held a long, bright sword in each of its four upper pincers, and its body was covered in scars, as if it had been in plenty of battles. Max guessed that it was the leader.

His heart was thumping as he walked up the icy beach to stand in front of the spider.

Its four sharp swords glittered, and Max saw that it also had razor-sharp jaws. It looked down at Max with eight tiny eyes that glinted like mirrors.

"Um... Thank you for helping us," he said in Aquoran. "We are on a Quest..."

The spider's scissor-like jaws moved together rapidly, making a clicking sound.

"Sorry," Max said. "I don't understand. Do you speak Aquoran? Or Merryn?"

"Hang on!" said Max's mum. She dived back into the *Leaping Dolphin* and re-emerged a few moments later, carrying a metal device that looked like a large shell, with a speaker built into it. "This is my Universal Translator – I managed to save it from the lab."

She set it in front of the huge spider, and Max began again.

"Thanks for saving us. We're looking for a rare metal called Rullium..." As he spoke, the

Translator emitted a series of rapid clicks.

The spider bent lower, listening. Max saw eight tiny images of himself reflected in its eyes.

The spider spoke again, and after a moment's delay, the Translator turned the sounds into Aquoran.

"My name is Anthrix, Captain of the Guard. Time will tell whether your thanks are fitting. But you are here, as expected."

*As expected?* Max thought with a frown. *What does he mean by that?*

"We will take you to the city," Anthrix said. "Our Emperor will want to meet you."

*At least that made sense*, Max thought.

"We will be glad to meet your Emperor," he said.

"That is fortunate, because you have no choice," Anthrix said. Max heard a soft clicking noise from the other spiders, almost as if they were laughing.

Lia turned and called out to her pet swordfish. "Don't worry, Spike! Stay there, and we'll be back soon!"

The spider army started crunching their way up the beach again. Max, Lia, Max's mother and Rivet followed, stumbling across the icy stones, with two spiders on either side and Anthrix behind them. *Almost as if he doesn't want us to get away*, Max thought. The submarine brought up the rear, grating noisily as it was pulled over the beach by four spiders.

As they drew nearer to the white haze, Max saw that it wasn't mountains in the distance at all. It was a city, made of huge structures of steely white spider-silk. There were spires, towers, citadels, all woven in intricate patterns, covered in ice which reflected the sunlight. It was dazzling.

The spiders kept up a rapid pace, and soon the ice buildings were looming all around them. *It's like walking through a maze of mirrors*, thought Max. They saw their own images reflected in panes of ice all around them, so it looked as if they were coming to meet themselves. Max couldn't tell how big

the city was; it seemed to go on forever.

"I've heard stories of this place," Max's mother whispered. "The Island of Illusion, they call it. I always thought it was a myth. But then I thought the Lost Lagoon was a myth, too."

More of the giant spiders were scuttling up and down the webbed buildings. Their white bodies were camouflaged against the shining white, but Max could see their shadows. He was aware of thousands of tiny glittering eyes watching him – but it was very difficult to tell what were eyes, and what was just light bouncing off the web.

It made him uneasy.

"What do you think Anthrix meant when he said he expected us?" he asked Lia, who was walking beside him.

Lia shrugged. "Probably a fault in that translator thing," she said.

"I don't know…the spiders don't know about Cora. Or the Robobeasts. Do they?"

"I doubt it," Lia said. "Or they'd have mentioned it. But we can tell them. Maybe they'll help us against Cora. I think these spiders would be pretty good to have on our side in a fight!"

The marching spiders stopped suddenly.

"This is the Emperor's palace," Anthrix said. Max could see the pride in the way the spider stood up straighter.

Max had to throw his head way back to see the top of the palace. It was dizzyingly high, with turrets and spires and bridges, all woven into incredibly beautiful patterns, white and shining. It looked as if it was made of lace.

"Prepare to meet the Emperor," said Anthrix.

# CHAPTER FIVE

# A FIGHT TO THE DEATH

Anthrix and two other spiders led them through the high palace doors, while the rest of the spiders waited outside with the *Leaping Dolphin*.

They stepped into a long, wide corridor, with walls of web and ice, carved into fantastic patterns of swirls and spirals. The spiders' feet clicked on the icy floor. It was very cold, and Max's breath came out in clouds of steam.

At the far end was a huge round chamber.

"Wow!" said Max as they entered.

"Impressive," his mother murmured.

Max marvelled at the smooth, highly polished walls of ice. He could see hundreds of reflections of himself, his mother, Lia and Rivet on every side and even, far off and tiny, on the domed ceiling.

Max heard a series of clicks. "Welcome!" came the voice from the Translator device that his mother carried. At the end of the chamber was a giant spider's web. And in the middle, with legs splayed right across the web, was the biggest spider Max had seen so far. It wore a crown of ice on its great round head.

"This is the realm of Colossia," the spider said. "And I am the Emperor of the Colossids."

"Pleased to meet you," said Max's mother.

"What brings you here?" the Emperor demanded, looking down at them.

"We're looking for a mineral called Rullium," Max said. "But we only want it to help us get out of here." He felt tense. No one had harmed them so far – in fact, the Colossids had saved them. But something about this city felt…creepy. It was hard to forget that they had nothing but a bent hyperblade for protection, and were surrounded by four giant Colossids, not to mention an army of them outside the palace.

"You were very fortunate," the Emperor said, "that one of our patrols spotted your undersea craft. We are an honourable race and always help those who come to us in need."

"Your Captain of the Guard said you were expecting us," Max said. "What did he mean?"

The Emperor continued as if he had not heard. "We can show you where to find the Rullium you need. But first, I offer you a tour of our island. There is much to admire."

"I'd rather just have the Rullium now," Lia

whispered. "We still have two more metals to find after that!"

"Come on, Lia," said Max's mum. "I'm sure the tour will be fascinating. Besides, the *Leaping Dolphin* needs repairs."

"We will begin by showing you our weapons forge," the Emperor said.

The weapons forge was underneath the palace, down a steep flight of ice steps. It was built of stone, and a massive furnace blazed at one end. For the first time since he had landed on the island, Max felt warm.

The Emperor and Anthrix stood behind them, as if guarding the door. Next to the furnace was another Colossid, whose body was a mottled reddish-brown, darkened by the flames. He was hunched over the fire, turning a glowing blade this way and that.

All around the forge hung weapons: steely

swords and scimitars, sabres and spears, gleaming red in the firelight.

"Wow!" Max murmured. "These spiders must really love fighting."

Lia nodded. "I said they'd be good to have on our side."

"All my soldiers are armed with weapons forged here," the Emperor said.

That gave Max an idea. He held up his bent, blunted hyperblade. "You wouldn't be able to fix this, would you?"

"Blacksmith," said the Emperor, "see what you can do to help."

The blacksmith spider scuttled forward and took the hyperblade from Max. He held it up to his eyes, scanning it carefully.

"Good quality," he said. "Pure vernium. This damage could only have been caused by another hyperblade, also of vernium."

"That's right," Max said. "Can you mend it?"

"Of course," said the blacksmith. He took the hyperblade in a pair of tongs and held it in the furnace. It glowed first red, then yellow, then white.

He placed the white-hot hyperblade on the anvil, took a great hammer, and beat it back into shape. *Clang! Clang! Clang!* Then he sharpened the blade on a huge stone wheel. Finally he plunged it into a bucket of iced water. There was a hiss and clouds of steam arose.

The blacksmith handed it back to Max.

"Thanks!" said Max, gazing at the blade. It looked brand new and sharper than ever.

Lia looked impressed. "I have a request," she said, approaching the Emperor. "You said you always help those in need. Would you be able to help us fight Cora Blackheart? She's an evil pirate who is trying to take over the whole ocean, and she's got these Robobeasts – sort of technological monsters – fighting for her. You are a race of warriors. If we had you on our side—"

The Emperor clicked louder than usual.

"Silence, child!" the Translator roared. "It is for the Emperor to offer help, not for you to demand it!"

Max and Lia shrank back, exchanging an awkward look: *Okay, then.*

There was a pause, and then the Emperor said calmly, as if Lia had never asked anything, "Yes, all our weapons are forged here. You were looking for Rullium? Look up." He pointed with a pincer.

Max looked up and noticed a long sword hanging from the ceiling. It was dazzling white and tapered to a needle-like point.

"That sword belonged to our most famous warrior and explorer," the Emperor said. "It is made of pure Rullium."

"It's beautiful," said Max's mother. "Obviously, we can't ask you to give us that! But is there any other source of Rullium on the island?"

"All in good time," the Emperor said. "Our tour is not over. Next up: the Arena."

The Arena was in the open air, a short distance from the city. They had to cross a wide, empty ice field to reach it. A cold wind blew, chilling Max to the bone. As they approached, he heard a chorus of clicking coming from the Arena. The clicking got louder and louder as they drew near.

The Colossids led them to the edge of a deep pit carved in the ice. *As big as the Aqua Sports Stadium back on Aquora*, Max thought. The sloping sides of the pit had been carved into seats. And in the seats sat thousands of Colossids, clicking their jaws excitedly. They were watching two Colossids down in the centre of the pit, locked in combat.

Max gasped at the sight. Both spiders fought standing on their four hind legs, the other four gripping swords and spears in their pincers. The weapons clanged and clashed together, sending sparks flying into the freezing air.

Max's gaze wandered to a large stand on the other side of the Arena – a viewing platform under a crimson canopy. It seemed to be empty at the moment, but Max guessed that was where the Emperor sat to watch these combats.

His mother shook her head. "That looks so dangerous! Like a real fight."

"It is a real fight," Anthrix said. "A fight to the death."

"What?" Max said. "But why?"

"For the spectators, it is sport," the Emperor said. "For the warriors, honour and glory."

Lia looked disgusted. "That's horrible!" she said.

As Max watched, one of the spiders in the Arena swung its sword wide, cutting two of its opponent's legs clean off. The other

Colossid staggered and fell. The victorious fighter placed one of its feet where its fallen opponent's head and thorax joined. It raised a spear, then looked towards the Emperor's box, as if asking permission to strike the death blow.

A figure appeared there, and Max froze.

Not a spider. A woman. Cora Blackheart. And she was grinning evilly.

She held out her arm and put her thumb down.

The victorious spider slashed down with his spear, cutting off the defeated spider's head. Lia let out a stunned cry and Max felt his stomach turn. Yellow blood ran out onto the ice.

The clicking of the crowd rose in a crescendo as the Emperor turned back to his visitors, mandibles clicking eagerly.

"Now it is your turn," he said.

# CHAPTER SIX

# TRAGG THE ICE BEAR

"Absolutely not!" snapped Max's mother. Her face was ablaze with anger. "You can't make us fight!"

"We can make you enter the arena," said Anthrix, "where you must fight to stay alive."

A steep slope of ice, cut between the tiered seats, led down to the arena. Anthrix and the two spider-guards pointed their spears at Max, his mother and Lia, herding them towards the slope.

Rivet planted himself in front of Anthrix, legs wide apart, barking furiously. But the spider just flicked one of his long legs at Rivet's chest, flipping the dogbot head over heels and sending him skittering down the ice slope, still barking madly.

"Rivet!" Max shouted.

"You had better go and join him," Anthrix said. He pushed Max with the tip of a spear, and Max had no choice but to edge back. Suddenly the ground disappeared from under his feet and he went hurtling down the ice-slide into the arena.

A couple of seconds later he hit the ground hard, rolled and got up, rubbing his knee where he'd banged it on the slide. A moment later he saw Lia and his mum come tumbling down the slope to join him.

Lia and his mum stood up and the three of them huddled together with Rivet in the centre of the arena. The dead Colossid lay on the ground nearby, in a pool of yellow blood. The victorious Colossid had disappeared. *So who will we be facing?* thought Max.

The crowd's excited clicking rose in volume.

"Max! No like, Max," said Rivet.

"Me neither," Max said.

"We've been double-crossed!" Max's mother fumed. "Those spiders were working for Cora all along! She must have driven us here with her Robobeasts, while she raced ahead on the aquabike and got here before us."

"Now what happens?" Lia said.

"We have to fight," Max said. "Lucky I got this fixed!" He held up his hyperblade, and it gleamed in the wintry sunlight.

Lia sprinted over to the dead Colossid and took the smallest of its spears from between its pincers. Judging by the loud clicking, the crowd seemed to like that.

Two Colossids scuttled out from a side door and dragged the dead body away. High up above, Cora stood. She was wearing a visor over her eyes with a microphone attachment – the Robobeast control unit. Her voice echoed through the arena.

"Now it's your turn to fight! Will you achieve glory – or death?" She cackled. "I wouldn't bet on glory if I were you! And make no mistake: once you are dead, I will escape from here, capture Aquora, and rule over all of Nemos!"

Max could feel his heart pounding in fury. "You'll never rule Nemos!" he shouted back. "We're not dead yet!" Then he turned to his mother and Lia. "Let's stand with our backs together, so we can defend in every direction!"

They did as he said, all facing outwards. Max's mum squeezed his hand.

"This is a tight spot," she said. "But we'll come through if we work together. I hope."

"Before the combat begins," Cora announced, "there's a little something I want. Dr North, that green brooch you're wearing – I'd hate see it covered in blood. Hand it over!"

The clicking from the crowd got louder and Max looked around, wondering what was exciting them. He saw that a door had opened in the side of the Arena. As he watched, four Colossids marched out.

Max swallowed hard and gripped the hilt of his hyperblade. *This is it.* If he had to die, he'd fight to the last!

But these Colossids didn't seem to want to fight. They walked over and stopped in front of Max's mother, and one held out its pincer.

"Give him the brooch!" commanded Cora.

Rivet barked defiantly at the Colossids. *That's weird*, thought Max. *What does Cora want a bit of jewellery for?*

Max's mother put her hand up and covered the brooch. "You can't have it!"

A flash of green, exactly the same shade as the brooch, flickered over her eyes. Max frowned, puzzled. *Could it have been a trick of the light? Maybe a reflection of the gem?*

The giant spiders stopped, suddenly seeming uncertain.

"Take the brooch!" shouted Cora.

"No," said Max's mother, still clutching the

brooch, her eyes still flashing green. "You're not getting it! Go away!"

To Max's amazement, the spiders obeyed. They inched their way backwards across the arena, moving mechanically, as if entranced.

"What are you doing?" Cora shrieked at the spiders. "Get the brooch! I want it!"

The Colossids continued to retreat through the door they had used to enter.

"How did you do that, Mum?" Max asked, staring at his mother.

She turned to Max, and he could see that her eyes were now back to their normal colour. "I don't know," she said with a shrug. "I didn't think they'd actually obey me!"

"Very well!" Cora said. "If I have to take the brooch from your dead body, then that's what I'll do!"

*Why does she want my mum's brooch so badly?* Max wondered.

Beside him, Lia shifted impatiently. She thumped the butt of her spear in the ground.

"Come on then!" she shouted up to Cora. "Let's get it over with. We're ready to fight some spiders!"

Cora Blackheart laughed. "Spiders? Oh, you won't be fighting spiders! You don't get it, do you? You're only here because my Robobeasts chased you here! The Colossids agreed to follow my plan, in exchange for new weaponry. They love weapons, these spiders! And they were particularly impressed with my new Robobeast, which you'll be fighting. Tell me – what do you think?"

The door at the side of the Arena swung open again. Max heard a low growling noise, and his blood froze.

A huge shape lumbered out into the arena. It was a bear, but by far the biggest Max had ever seen. It made even the Colossids look

weak and spindly.

Its fur was bright blue, covered in places with gleaming silver armour. It had metal plates over its neck, back and shoulders, and a metal helmet on its head. Its eyes glowed an angry red. Max saw wires sticking out from the armour plating, joining under its neck.

He wiped his brow, struggling to look calm, not wanting Cora to see how she'd rattled him. He had battled plenty of scary Robobeasts. But few had given such a terrifying impression of raw power. He heard his mother draw in her breath, and felt Lia tense beside him. Rivet was barking again, but now his bark sounded scared and high-pitched.

"I call him Tragg the Ice Bear!" Cora called out. "Isn't that a sweet name?"

Tragg roared, and the mighty sound seemed to shake the whole arena.

The crowd clicked their mandibles and began to clash their swords together in excitement.

Before Max could say anything to Lia or his mum, the bear lowered its head and charged.

It moved at incredible speed. Max and the others scattered as the Robobeast thundered by, so close that Max felt the wind caused by its heavy paws passing over his back.

Tragg half rose onto its hind legs, turned and lunged at Max again.

Max ducked and swiped at the bear with his hyperblade, but the blade just bounced off the armour plating.

From the corner of his eye Max saw Cora speaking into the microphone on her headset. *She must be controlling it*, Max thought.

The bear opened its huge mouth wide, and its throat glittered with metal. *There's some kind of technological implant in there*, Max realised, *some kind of weapon*. Something was going to come out of that metallic throat. Something dangerous…

He dived to the ground.

A great white spray of freezing ice crystals blasted out from the bear's mouth. A pile of ice instantly collected on the spot where Max had been standing, big enough to have covered Max from head to foot. *I'd have been frozen to death in a heartbeat*, Max thought.

Before he could pick himself up, the Robobeast charged again. Max rolled clear as fast as he could, but the tips of its claws raked his forearm. Blood spurted out onto the icy ground. He dropped the hyperblade.

Tragg reared up above him…

"No!" Max heard his mother cry.

Lia suddenly ran in front of Tragg, jabbing at its stomach with her spear. The bear swiped at her with its mighty paw. She leaped aside – but Max just had time to get up and move clear. He clutched at his wounded arm. It hurt like crazy, but there was no time to worry about that now.

Cora laughed, and began murmuring into her microphone again.

Tragg swung around to face Max's mother. Slowly, menacingly, it padded towards her.

*Oh no you don't*, Max thought. Usually his mother was more than capable of defending herself, but now she was unarmed.

She backed away.

Max snatched up his hyperblade.

The Robobeast growled, speeding up.

Max stared at the beast, his heart filling with anger as it drove his mother further back, back, back towards the Arena wall.

Suddenly Lia ran at Tragg again, stabbing the bear with her spear, just under its armour. But its fur was too thick for the blade to find purchase. The spear snapped in half, not even drawing blood.

Max's mother had her back to the wall now. He could see fear in her eyes. *No, no, no…*

The bear opened its mouth wide.

Max started to run.

But he was too far away.

*I'm not going to get there in time to save her!*

# CHAPTER SEVEN

# ESCAPE FROM THE ARENA

Max felt like he was running in slow motion. He saw his mother raise her hands to shield her face as Tragg opened his great mouth, ready to blast out a deadly gale of icy breath...

A flash of silver came hurtling out of nowhere, knocking Max's mother aside. Rivet! But Max's joy turned to shock as the icy blast of Tragg's breath hit the dogbot full on.

*CLANG!* Rivet hit the ground, already

frozen solid. Ice crystals had formed all over his
metal body.

The watching Colossids hissed excitedly.

"This is fun!" shouted Cora. "Who's next? You
can run, but you can't hide!"

Max's cheeks flushed hot with rage. Cora was
pure evil! There was no way he was going to let
her triumph like this.

His mother ran to his side, followed by Lia.

Tragg swung its snout towards them. Its head alone was bigger than a man. Its eyes flashed red, and its mouth opened in a roar, revealing teeth like curved knives in front of the ice spray. *The ice spray...*

"Listen," Max said urgently. "Cora's right about one thing, there's nowhere to hide. But I've got a plan to get us out of here. We can use Tragg's own weapon against it. Follow me!"

He sprinted to the wall. It rose high over his head, much too high to climb. *Unless...*

"Hey, Tragg!" he called. "Come and get me!"

Tragg turned to fix him with its red glare, then padded towards him, slow and threatening.

The audience went quiet. *Probably wondering if I've given up*, thought Max.

The bear opened its great mouth and Max leaped to one side as its ice breath blasted out.

As he clambered to his feet, he turned to see that a pile of ice roughly the size of Rivet had formed against the wall. *Yes! It's working...*

"Right!" Lia said with a smile. "I get it!"

She threw the broken half of her spear at Tragg, but it bounced harmlessly off a metal plate. Unfazed, Lia jumped on top of the ice pile. "Come and get me, you stupid fat bear!"

Again, Tragg roared out its deadly, freezing breath. Lia jumped nimbly out of the way as more crystals piled on top of the ice heap, raising it higher still.

Tragg turned to chase Lia – but as it did so, Max's mother climbed on top of the frozen pile. She scooped up a handful of ice and flung it at the bear's face. "You're not trying, Tragg! Have another go!" she said.

The bear turned back with a roar, and blasted out one more stream of ice crystals. But Max's mum had already jumped clear.

At last the heap of ice reached to the top of the pit wall.

"Let's get out of here!" Max said. "I'll distract the bear!" He clanged his hyperblade on the frozen ground. "Come on, Tragg – let's see what you've got!"

The bear began to lumber towards him, growling. Max cast a quick glance to see his mother climbing up the ice slope and over the wall. Lia scrambled up after her.

Now it was Max's turn. He just had to get past Tragg first.

"Enough fooling around!" Cora screamed. "Tragg – eat him!"

The bear roared, and sprang at Max.

Max dived forward, between the Robobeast's front paws and under its body. As the bear leaped over his head, Max stabbed upwards with his hyperblade, and it clanged against the bear's armour plating. The noise coming from underneath it seemed to confuse the Robobeast. It landed, reared up on its hind legs and looked around for Max.

Max was already running for the ice heap. "Don't worry, Riv – I'll be back for you!" he shouted, although he didn't know whether Rivet could hear him. He half climbed, half ran up the ice and followed Lia and his mother up the stand of seating. The Colossids shrank away as they passed, clearly taken aback.

"Let's make for the forge!" Max's mother panted. "We'll get the Rullium sword and get out of here!"

There was a thunderous roar behind them.

Max glanced back and saw that Cora had leaped down from her platform and was now riding on Tragg's back. She and the bear came leaping up out of the Arena in pursuit. "You'll never get away!" she screamed, furious.

The Colossids in the audience scattered in a

panic. Max could feel the tiered seating shake under the Robobeast's immense weight. Cora rose up and cracked her electronic cat-o'-nine-tails, laughing horribly.

*There's no way we can take on Tragg and Cora together,* Max thought. *We have to stay ahead of them. Somehow...*

They reached the top of the stand and came

out onto the flat plain, with the City of Illusion in the distance. It was too far away – there was no way they could get there before the bear caught up. Its roars grew louder behind them, and Max heard Cora cackling in triumph.

Then Max spotted Cora's aquabike – the one she'd stolen from him. She had fitted it with ski-runners, he saw, but apart from that it was just the same as when he'd last had it.

*Perfect.*

"Jump on!" he said to Lia and his mum. They leaped aboard as Max threw himself into the driving seat and twisted the throttle.

The bike jolted forward. Back in the saddle, Max felt at home straight away. He skimmed the bike smoothly over the ice, racing towards the city. Towards the palace and the forge.

But even above the noise of the engine, Max could hear Tragg roaring. The Robobeast was fast. And it was gaining on them.

The city loomed up before them, and all at once they were weaving between the tall structures, the towers and the spires and the monuments of glistening white web.

Max heard Tragg behind them, smashing through the buildings. *That has to slow it down a bit*, Max thought. *At least, I hope it does...*

Colossids ran out into the streets. Others came climbing down their giant webs, waving swords and spears. But they weren't trying to stop Max. It looked like they'd finally decided that the Robobeast smashing up their city, and the woman riding it, were the real enemies.

Max turned in his saddle and saw the giant spiders swipe at the bear with their weapons, but it knocked them aside. Others tried to catch it in webs they flung out as it passed. But it broke through the strands easily.

"Work together!" yelled Max. "If you hit it with your webs all at the same time, you might stop it!"

"Watch where you're going!" Lia screamed.

Max spun round and saw the webbed wall of a building right ahead. He hit the brake and swerved, just skidding past.

But the loss of speed was all it took for Tragg

to gain on them. A stream of ice gusted out in front of the aquabike, solidifying into a ramp, just in time for the bike to slam straight into it. Max felt the aquabike climb steeply into the air, out of his control. The handlebars were wrenched from his grasp and the bike flipped over, sending its passengers flying.

Max hit the icy ground with a thump, sliding a little way. Fighting for breath, he fumbled for the hyperblade at his belt. Any second Tragg would be upon him.

He looked up and gasped.

Tragg was standing over Max's mother where she had fallen on the ice. Its massive paws were on her shoulders, pinning her down. She was helpless.

From high up on the giant bear's back, Cora sneered at Max's mother.

"Shall I kill you and then take the brooch?" she said. "Or shall I take it and then kill you?"

# CHAPTER EIGHT

# HYPERBLADE VERSUS CAT-O'-NINE-TAILS

"I think I'll take the brooch first," Cora said. "I want to see the look in your eyes when you know I've won. *Then* I'll kill you."

Max scrambled to his feet, took hold of the aquabike's handlebars and jerked it upright. Cora wasn't looking at him. She was hanging over the bear's shoulder and reaching down for the brooch. "Come on, let's have it!"

Max's heart raced. Cora and the bear were

perfectly positioned, just in front of the ramp of ice. He revved the engine and drove up the ramp, twisting the throttle as far as it would go. Cora looked round in alarm as the aquabike flew through the air towards her. Max closed his eyes and braced himself...

*CRRUMMMPPP!*

The bike crashed into the side of Tragg, the impact jolting every bone in Max's body and

sending Cora flying. Max held on tight as the bike crashed to the ground and landed on its runners.

Tragg remained standing over Max's mother, like a block of stone, waiting for its next order. Max leaped off his bike and raced over to Cora. She had risen to her knees when he reached her. He drew his hyperblade and held it to her throat.

"Call the bear off!" he ordered.

"Or what?" sneered Cora.

"Just do it!" Max said.

"You wouldn't kill me!" Cora said. "You don't have the guts, boy!"

"You tried to kill my mother!" Max said fiercely. He pressed the hyperblade a little harder against Cora's neck. "Do you want to take the risk?"

Cora glared at Max. A long moment passed. The hilt of the blade grew slippery with sweat.

Then Cora breathed deeply, looked away and spoke into her headset. "Back off, Tragg."

The huge bear stepped backwards, growling softly. Max breathed a sigh of relief as his mother got up, rubbing her shoulders where the bear's paws had pressed. She looked dishevelled but unharmed. "Thanks, Max," she said shakily.

Lia came running across. "Nice work, Max! What shall we do with Cora now?"

"I don't know," said Max. "Tie her up with something, maybe—"

There was a sudden noise of scrabbling and clicking. Max looked up to see a group of Colossids scuttling towards them. They were hissing and throwing spears at Tragg. Some bounced off his armour, others stuck in his fur. Immediately the bear roared and charged the Colossids. It smashed one with its paw. They scattered, but Anthrix and two other

Colossids returned to the attack, jabbing at the bear with their swords.

"I have an idea!" Max said. "Go and tell the Colossids to work together to build a web to trap the Robobeast."

Niobe and Lia ran towards the spiders. Suddenly Max felt a violent push against his chest, and he tumbled to the ground. *No! I shouldn't have taken my eyes off Cora...* Before Max could regain his balance, Cora snatched up one of the spears that had been hurled. Then she pulled out her electric cat-o'-nine-tails.

She smiled and advanced on Max, a weapon in each hand.

"I always enjoy killing people," she said. "But I'm especially going to enjoy killing you."

Feeling desperate, Max darted forward with the hyperblade, trying to knock the spear from Cora's hand.

The cat-o'-nine-tails swished and wrapped itself around Max's arm, and a wave of unbelievable pain surged through him. His arm felt as if it had been plunged into boiling water.

Somehow he managed to keep hold of his hyperblade, and parry Cora's next spear-lunge. But he didn't know how much longer he could hold her off. She was a deadly fighter, and better armed than he was.

Cora twirled the cat-o'-nine-tails above her head.

Behind her, Tragg and the spiders were still fighting, but Tragg seemed to be getting the better of it. Max also saw that Lia and his mother were with a group of the Colossids, directing them to spin a thick web between two buildings.

"Hey, Cora!" Max said. "Look behind you!"

Cora laughed. "I'm not about to fall for that one!"

The cat-o'-nine-tails scythed down, and Max dived to one side. He rolled and jumped to his feet in time to block another spear-thrust with his hyperblade.

"Getting tired, Max?" Cora said, smiling. "Why not just give up now?"

"Never!"

Cora flailed the electric whip at him again.

He jumped back, slipped on the ice and fell heavily.

"I thought you'd put up a better fight than that," Cora said as she stood over him. "I'm disappointed in you."

She raised her spear.

Tragg and Anthrix were still locked in combat. The bear was driving the giant spider back, towards Cora and Max. The fight came closer, and closer...

"You really should look behind you," Max said.

"I've already told you," sneered Cora, "that trick's not going to work."

Tragg and Anthrix were right behind Cora now. Too late, she heard the spider's legs scrabbling on the ice and spun round. One of Anthrix's legs struck her a glancing blow. The spear flew from her hand and the headset was knocked off her head.

Max jumped to his feet, darting aside to avoid being trampled by the furious fighting Beasts.

Cora scrabbled over the ice for her headset and jammed it back on her head. "Tragg!" she commanded. "Leave the spider – get the boy. Kill him!"

Tragg immediately stopped trying to bite Anthrix's legs off and lumbered towards Max, picking up speed.

Max ran in a loop right around the bear and started to sprint back towards the web the Colossids had prepared. *If only I can stay ahead of Tragg for long enough!*

He could hear the bear's fast, padding footsteps on the icy ground behind him. It was gaining.

*If I can just make it to the web...*

"Come on, Max!" he heard Lia shout. "You can do it!"

Max heard a change in the bear's foosteps. They were getting closer together. In horror, he realised...it was getting ready to spring!

*Are we close enough?* Max wasn't sure. But he was out of time. He threw himself flat.

The bear went sailing over his head and crashed into the web. It bounced, swayed, wriggled, snarled. It thrashed around madly.

But the giant web held the Robobeast fast.

Max's mum and Lia cheered. The Colossids clashed their swords together in celebration.

Max got up. His heart was beating fast and he was covered in sweat. He looked back to see what Cora was doing.

She was staring at them. Even in the distance, Max thought he could see the expression of disgust on her face. Then she jumped on his aquabike and skimmed away across the ice.

"She knows she can't fight us all," Max's mother said. "Not without the bear!"

"Can't we go after her?" Lia said.

"I wish we could," Max said. "But we'd never catch her. Not when she's on that bike."

Anthrix came stalking back in their direction. He stopped in front of Tragg, still struggling in the web.

"That bear must die," he said, twirling all four of his swords around.

"No!" said Max. "Don't kill it! It's not really evil – Cora Blackheart's been controlling it."

"But it's dangerous," Anthrix said.

"Max can easily reprogram it," said Max's mother. "Can't you, Max?"

"Oh, thanks, Mum!" said Max.

He moved cautiously towards the web, hoping that his mother was right.

"Watch out!" Lia said. "Don't let it freeze you!"

"That's the plan," Max said.

He climbed onto the web, staying out of reach of Tragg's mouth. It snarled, showing its teeth, twisting its head to get at him. It sent a shiver down Max's spine.

"Come on Max," called his mother. "You can do it. Reprogram it!"

"Actually, I've got a better idea," Max said. He grabbed the wires that ran from Tragg's helmet to underneath its neck. "It's easier just to pull them out!" He tugged hard, and the wires came away in a shower of sparks.

The red light in Tragg's eyes died. Its armour plating came loose and tumbled to earth with a series of clangs. It coughed, and the silver freeze-gun clattered out onto the ice.

Max jumped down, scrubbing bits of web off himself.

Lia picked up a fallen sword and sliced through the web to free the bear.

It fell to the ground, standing up on its four paws again. It stretched and shook itself, as if awaking from a long nap, then stared at Max for one long moment.

"I think it's grateful," Max's mum murmured. But she didn't have to tell Max. He could see it in the bear's eyes.

The next moment it was running away across the ice, towards the sea, its blue fur bright and vivid against the white landscape.

# CHAPTER NINE

# THE RULLIUM SWORD

"Take this," the Emperor of the Colossids said, bending down and handing the Rullium sword to Max, "with our thanks."

Max took the sword and swished it through the air. It seemed to weigh almost nothing and the blade flashed radiantly white.

They were standing in the great forge. Rivet had thawed out next to the furnace, and he lay there wagging his tail and giving an occasional sneeze.

"It's amazing," Max said. "Thanks!"

"It is no more than you deserve," the Emperor said. "You and your friends fought with great bravery. I see now that we sided with the wrong person."

"That's all right," Max's mother said.

Lia sniffed but said nothing.

"We must be on our way," Max's mum

said. "We've still got two metals to find!"

"Your vessel is ready," the Emperor said. "Follow me."

He led Max, Max's mother, Lia and Rivet out of the forge. The *Leaping Dolphin* was outside, sitting on a big sledge on the ice. Max smiled when he saw it.

"It looks as good as new!" Niobe said.

"My blacksmith worked on it," the Emperor said. "After you had repaired the engine and recharged the batteries, he scraped all the rock away and filled the holes with molten metal."

"Nice job," Max's mother said. She patted the hull. "I'm looking forward to travelling in her again!"

Lia sighed. "I'm not!"

"We'd better get going," Max said. "We have to find the last two metals before Cora can stop us!"

"My guards will escort you to the coast," the Emperor said. "Goodbye, and thank you."

Anthrix and a group of armed Colossids marched with them down to the sea, with four of the spiders dragging the *Leaping Dolphin* on its sledge. As they neared the water, Spike jumped out, flapping his fins at them in delight. Lia splashed straight into the sea and hugged him.

The Colossids pushed the *Leaping Dolphin* into the water. Max and his mother climbed on top, then stood and waved to the Colossids on the shore.

Anthrix raised one of his jointed limbs in a military salute.

Max took one last look at the beautiful, white, shimmering Island of Illusion. Then he followed his mother down into the sub.

Soon they had left the Island far behind, and were in open water again. The *Leaping Dolphin* was travelling fast, its engine humming smoothly. Through the porthole, Max saw Lia and Spike swimming along beside them in the grey water.

The Rullium sword lay on a shelf, next to the Galdium.

"That's two of them!" Max's mother said,

following his gaze. "Two more to go! Then we can make our compass and get out of the Lost Lagoon."

"Where do we head to next?" Max asked.

"I'm not sure," Max's mum said. "But we'll find what we need. Somehow." Her hand went to the green brooch and stroked the edge of it.

*There's something strange about that brooch*, Max thought, remembering the flash of green he'd seen in his mum's eyes in the Arena. Why had Cora wanted it so badly?

And where was the pirate now? Was she near? Was she watching them? She still had at least two Robobeasts and the device to control them. If she got out of the Lagoon before they did, the whole ocean would be at her mercy.

But the *Leaping Dolphin* was back to its best. He had his hyperblade. And Lia and his mother were by his side.

If anyone could stop Cora Blackheart, it was them.

Don't miss Max's next Sea Quest
adventure, when he faces

# HORVOS
## THE HORROR BIRD

Look out for all the books in
Sea Quest Series 5:
# THE CHAOS QUADRANT

**SYTHID THE SPIDER CRAB**

**BRUX THE TUSKED TERROR**

**VENOR THE SEA SCORPION**

**MONOTH THE SPIKED DESTROYER**

## OUT IN APRIL 2015!

Don't miss the
**BRAND NEW**
Special Bumper Edition:
## DRAKKOS
## THE OCEAN KING

978 1 40832 848 4

## OUT IN NOVEMBER 2014

# WIN AN EXCLUSIVE GOODY BAG

In every Sea Quest book the Sea Quest logo is hidden in one of the pictures. Find the logos in books 13-16, make a note of which pages they appear on and go online to enter the competition at

## www.seaquestbooks.co.uk

Each month we will put all of the correct entries into a draw and select one winner to receive a special Sea Quest goody bag.

You can also send your entry on a postcard to:

Sea Quest Competition, Orchard Books, 338 Euston Road, London, NW1 3BH

Don't forget to include your name and address!

## GOOD LUCK

### Closing Date:  Nov 30th 2014

# DON'T MISS THE
# BRAND NEW SERIES OF:

## Series 15: VELMAL'S REVENGE

978 1 40833 487 4

978 1 40833 489 8

978 1 40833 491 1

978 1 40833 493 5

# COMING SOON!